A ViLe VaLeNTiNe!

BuzzPop

BuzzPop

An imprint of Bonnier Publishing USA

251 Park Avenue South, New York, NY 10010

Manufactured in China HOX 0918

First Edition 1 3 5 7 9 10 8 6 4 2

ISBN 978-1-4998-0680-9

buzzpopbooks.com

bonnierpublishingusa.com

Under license by:

©2018 Moose Enterprise (INT) Pty Ltd. Grossery Gang™ logos, names, and characters are licensed trademarks of Moose Enterprise (INT) Pty Ltd.

29 Grange Road, Cheltenham, VIC 3192, Australia

www.moosetoys.com

info@moosetoys.com

Putrid Pizza was surprised to see Squished Banana and Blue Spew Cheese peering out from a huge mountain of trash in the Yucky Mart.

"What's cookin'?" Pizza Face asked.

"It's Valentine's Day," called out Ricardo, "so we're looking for a box of candy."

"Found one," cried Stinky as he flung the box into the air. *CRASH!* It landed right on top of Pizza Face, knocking him down.

When Pizza Face opened his eyes, the first thing he saw was a pile of trash.

"I'm in love," he sighed, looking up at the steaming, rotting garbage.

"Awesome!" cried Blew Spew Cheese. "Pizza Face's mind's finally rotted, just like his cheese!"

"Not true!" replied Ricardo, the King of Romance. "He's fallen under a magical Valentine's Day spell. He's in love!"

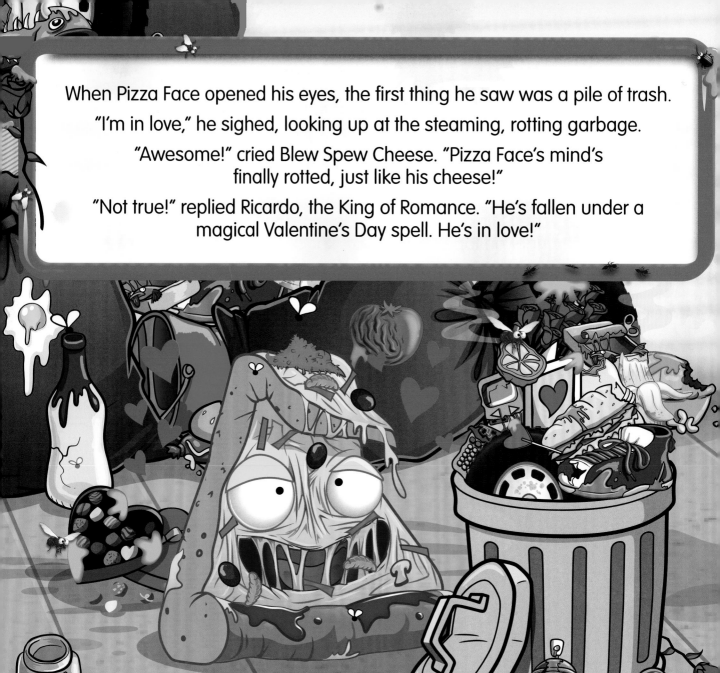

Pizza Face swooned in front of the rotting trash. "I love you, you sweet-smelling, decaying heap of garbage."

But the overflowing garbage can did not seem to share his feelings.

"Help me win the heart of this stunning stinker!" cried Pizza Face to the King of Romance.

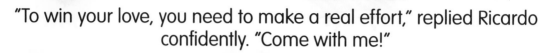

"To win your love, you need to make a real effort," replied Ricardo confidently. "Come with me!"

Ricardo gave Pizza Face a fancy outfit and gifts for the trash pile. Then he presented the new and improved Pizza Face to his love.

"Ta-da!" said Ricardo, but the trash pile seemed unimpressed by Pizza Face's makeover.

"Recite a poem," whispered Ricardo.

Pizza Face stood in front of the trash pile, cleared his throat, and began: "Roses are red, violets are blue, I thought I was the grossest, but then I saw you."

"That poem was rubbish!" said Stinky. He giggled, but Ricardo shushed him.

The trash said nothing.

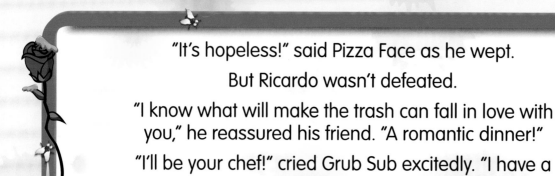

"It's hopeless!" said Pizza Face as he wept.

But Ricardo wasn't defeated.

"I know what will make the trash can fall in love with you," he reassured his friend. "A romantic dinner!"

"I'll be your chef!" cried Grub Sub excitedly. "I have a perfectly gross menu!"

As the sun set, Pizza Face sat outside the Yucky Mart, chewing rotting frogs legs and singing love songs to his beloved trash pile.

"I don't think Pizza Face has noticed that the trash hasn't eaten or said anything yet," Stinky said to Ricardo.

"Give it time!" replied Ricardo, the world's grossest romantic.

"And for the main course, we have my speciality: stinking green lobster with a sour cream worm sauce," announced Meathead.

"Yummy!" cried Pizza Face. "This is even more delicious than dried jelly beans with slime on top!"

Pizza Face gobbled it up.

"For dessert, we have steamed fungus pudding!" cried Meathead as he placed the disgusting slop on the table.

"My favorite!" oozed Pizza Face. "May I feed you a spoonful, my love?" Pizza Face asked the pile of trash.

Meathead couldn't take it anymore. "Don't throw away my food," he said. "That rotting lot can't appreciate my fine cuisine!"

"No one insults my trash!" screamed Pizza Face. He swept up the trash can into his arms. "Don't worry, my love. I'll take care of you," he whispered as he ran back inside the Yucky Mart.

"I told you his mind has rotted," said Stinky to Ricardo.

Ricardo was still determined that love would triumph.

"Let's have a Valentine's Day dance!" he suggested.

"Barf-tastic!" cried Dodgey Donut. "I'll organize the grossest romantic dance ever!"

In no time, music filled the Yucky Mart. All the Grossery Gang competed to see who had the best moves. Ricardo showed off his famous Banana Split and left a trail of slimy ooze on the floor.

"Watch me!" Pizza Face shouted as he jumped on a table and danced. Slugs dripped off his body as he shook violently.

"Get a load of my cheesy moves!" he said, confident his dancing would make the trash fall in love with him.

Just as Pizza Face moved in for a kiss,
Ricardo banana-slipped on his own trail of slimy ooze.
He crashed right into the couple, ruining the
romantic moment.

Pizza Face scrambled to stand up. He was furious.

"Ricardo!" he screamed. "You ruined my special moment! Why would you do that?"

Then Pizza Face got a crazy idea. "You haven't been helping me. You've been trying to sabotage me . . . because you're in love with the trash pile, too!"

"That's crazy!" cried Ricardo, but it was too late. Pizza Face had jumped on top of him. Bruised and full of ooze, Ricardo stretched out and grabbed a handful of garbage, hurling it at his angry friend.

"Garbage fight!" shouted Stinky. Immediately, the dancing stopped and the fighting began.

Soon the air was filled with flying, moldy garbage. The rotting liquids made the dance floor more like an ice rink, and the Grossery Gang laughed as they slipped across the floor.

"I'll take a trash fight over dancing any day!" said Meathead.

"Take that!" yelled Rocky as a rotting orange struck Pizza Face.

But just as he was about to grab a handful of garbage, Pizza Face suddenly realized with horror that everyone had been throwing the garbage from his beloved trash pile.

"My trash!" Pizza Face wept. "My love is spread all over the Yucky Mart." He tried frantically to pick up all the trash, but he failed to see the huge puddle of Ricardo's slime on the floor.

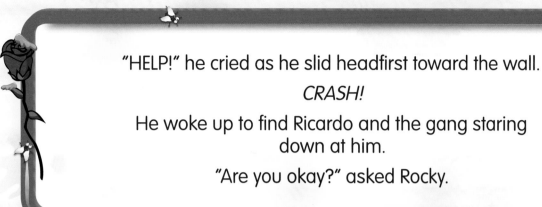

"HELP!" he cried as he slid headfirst toward the wall.

CRASH!

He woke up to find Ricardo and the gang staring down at him.

"Are you okay?" asked Rocky.